〔绘本中国故事系列〕

雪舟画鼠

杨永青／绘画　吕锡贞／文字

王一方／翻译

连环画出版社

北京

雪舟是画家，
学画留佳话。

XueZhou was a painter, his painting learning is a much told tale.

小时当和尚，
偷空就画画。

He was a monk at young age, taking his time off painting.

一天正画猫，师父把他罚。

One day his master punished him for painting a cat.

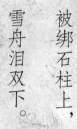

被绑石柱上，
雪舟泪双下。

He was tied up on a stone pillar with tears flowing down.

脚边一汪泪，
沾泪还可画。

Tears made a puddle beside his feet which could be painted with.

There was not enough tears for painting a cat, so he painted a mouse.

脚丫当画笔，
画得真不差。

He used his feet as a painting brush which worked well.

师父见泪鼠，
当成真鼠抓。

The master mistook the tear-mouse as a real one, and tried to catch it.

赶鼠鼠不走，
跺脚鼠不怕。

The mouse would not go away, neither sacred by stamping feet.

师父明白了，
鼠是徒弟画。

The master realized the mouse was painted by Xuezhou.

师父受感动，
解绳安慰他。

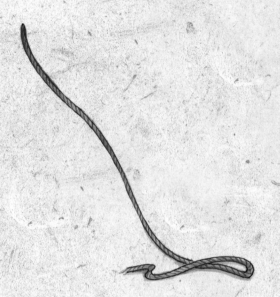

The master was moved by Xuezhou's talent, he untied him and comforted him.

「雪舟好孩子，以后尽管画。」

"Good boy, paint as you like."

师父买纸笔，
请师指导他。

The master bought him drawing paper and painting brushes;

he also found Xuezhou a teacher to guide him.

雪舟享盛名，
终成大画家。

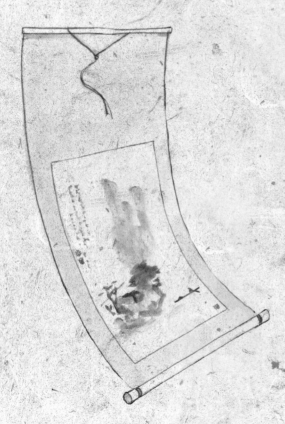

Eventually, Xuezhou became a famous painting artist.

图书在版编目（CIP）数据

雪舟画鼠：汉英对照 / 杨永青绘；吕锡贞文字
. -- 北京：连环画出版社，2016.10
（绘本中国故事系列）
ISBN 978-7-5056-3289-9

Ⅰ.①雪… Ⅱ.①杨… ②吕… Ⅲ.①儿童故事 – 图
画故事 – 中国 – 当代 Ⅳ.①I287.8

中国版本图书馆CIP数据核字(2016)第221804号

绘本中国故事 中英双语图画故事书

雪舟画鼠 xue zhou hua shu

编辑出版　连环画出版社
　　　　　（北京北总布胡同32号　邮编：100735）
　　　　　http://www.renmei.com.cn
　　　　　发行部：（010）67517601　（010）67517602
　　　　　邮购部：（010）67517797

绘　画　杨永青
文　字　吕锡贞
翻　译　王一方
责任编辑　李雪竹　张 煤　刘 柳
装帧设计　鲁明静
内文制作　汤 妮
责任校对　马晓婷
责任印制　刘建春
制版印刷　山东德州新华印务有限责任公司
经　销　全国新华书店

版　次：2016年11月　第1版　第1次印刷
开　本：889mm×1194mm　1/16
印　张：2.25
印　数：0001—3000册
ISBN 978-7-5056-3289-9
定　价：28.00元

启事：因时隔久远很遗憾与作者失去联系，希望作者与我社联系。